The Mystery of the Spaniel Family's Dog House

Written by
Sharon Ellsberry
Illustrated by
Amy Fox

The Mystery of the Spaniel Family's Dog House

Written by Sharon Ellsberry

Illustrated by Amy Fox

For Marguerite, Orville & Eva, Frank & Lucille

The Mystery of the Spaniel Family's Dog House

Story by Sharon Ellsberry

Illustrations, book design, and layout by Amy Fox

Summary:
Three Spaniel dogs (Joe, Daisy, and Maggie) discover what's been lurking in their dog house and from there another mystery about an old abandoned property unfolds.
(1.Dogs—Fiction. 2. Mystery—Fiction. 3. Texas—Fiction. 4. Humorous stories.)

Other works by the author include:

The Spaniel Family Goes to the State Fair

The Spaniel Family's Pen Pal Adventure

EEI
1006 Dove Creek Drive
Athens, Texas 75751
1-800-317-4804
Visit us at www.gospaniels.com

ISBN-13: 978-0-9790777-1-5

Printed in the U.S.A.
By Wheeler Press
www.wheelerpress.com

Contents

Chapter 1

Something was not Right

The Spaniel family didn't know what to think. Ever since their move to the pleasant little town in East Texas, it seemed their dog house was occupied by someone or something they couldn't see. The Spaniels wondered, "Did a ghost move into our house when we came here?" Every time Maggie, Joe, or Daisy tried to poke their heads in the doorway to take a peek inside, they heard something, or smelled something, or felt something that made them want to run. After several weeks of unusual noises and strange feelings, they decided they were no longer going to try to sleep in, or even go near, their dog house. The Spaniel pups spent their nights curled up on rugs on the kitchen floor. They felt safe in their owner's home, but their own dog house, in their backyard had them worried. It really was a shame.

During the day, the Spaniels romped and played, chased squirrels, and took naps in their backyard, but they made sure to avoid the dog house. When things were quiet and all was truly still, they could perk their ears and hear sounds coming from their house. They heard scratching, digging, low moans, and faint laughter. Sometimes, dirt flew out the front door of their dog house. There was no explanation for any of this. The dogs were frightened.

After months of mystery and weeks of wondering, one member of the Spaniel family was ready for answers. Maggie announced to brother Joe and sister Daisy, "I am sick and tired of being afraid and having my naps interfered with by the sounds coming from that house." Maggie had been reading the newspaper and saw an ad for a ghost hunter. She told Joe and Daisy, "It's time to call for help!"

Joe asked, "What will the ghost hunter do?"

Maggie replied, "Well, Joe, since none of us will go near our house, the ghost hunter will come and search it for us. If there is a ghost or some other spooky thing in there, the ghost hunter will find it and get rid of it."

Daisy barked, "Yea, we are going to get rid of the terrible thing in our dog house!"

Chapter 2
Ghost Hunter to the Rescue

The next day a massive bulldog carrying lots of flashlights, cameras, and other devices in his special backpack, popped his big head under the Spaniel family's fence. He squirmed and grunted as he wedged his bulky body beneath the biggest hole. Daisy quickly ran over to where the bulldog was attempting to enter. She dug feverishly to help the big canine come into their yard. Finally, the large dog worked his way under the fence and completely inside. He looked at Daisy and said, "Well, thanks so much little lady." Then, the bulldog slowly made his way toward Joe and Maggie. He panted as he waddled and let his long tongue hang loosely from his mouth. Drool from his droopy jowls dripped down and collected on the walkway and grass, leaving a sloppy trail.

The bulldog's entire body swayed with each step and wiggled long after he stopped moving.

Maggie stepped forward to greet the big dog. "Hello sir, my name is Maggie Spaniel. I'm the one who called you. This is my little brother Joe, with the chocolate colored fur, and my little sister Daisy, with the black fur. She's the one who helped you enter our yard."

"Pleased to meet y'all. My full name is Jaba the Mutt, but most folks just call me Jaba. Ghost hunting is my specialty. Now, what seems to be the trouble here?"

"Well, we believe we may have a haunted dog house. We keep hearing the oddest noises coming from it. This has been happening day and night for weeks."

"Can you describe those noises for me?" he asked.

"Well, sometimes we hear low moans, and we also hear scratching and steps. Strangely, we hear faint laughter coming from the house." Just after

Maggie said that, a tiny laugh could be heard trickling out the front door of their dog house.

Maggie barked, "Did you hear that?" Joe and Daisy began barking and howling. Big sister Maggie hushed the pups and everybody listened to see if the laughing would continue. Not a sound could be heard from anybody or from the dog house.

Jaba went to the door of their house and poked his big head in the dark opening. He sniffed the air and noticed a musty smell that reminded him of digging in dirt. The bulldog stood very still and listened for a few minutes. No scratching, digging, or laughter could be heard, but Jaba felt the strangest feeling. Was something watching him? His eyes saw nothing in the thick darkness. He thought, "There is something in this house and I'm going to find out what it is." Jaba abruptly pulled his head out of the doorway and said, "Ah ha... hump...I see...well...this is very interesting and I really can't wait to get started. I'll be back after midnight to search your home."

"Why then? Why don't you just finish your investigation now?" Maggie asked.

Jaba replied, "Ghost hunting is best late at night. It's their favorite time to haunt and frighten animals and people. I have the best chance of catching a glimpse of this thing that is scaring you after you go to bed. There is no need for you and your brother and sister to stay up for my return."

Maggie said, "Thank you so much, sir. We will just go ahead and sleep on our safe kitchen floor inside our owner's home."

Jaba barked, "I'll be back later. Don't worry about a thing. Investigating is what I do, and I'm mighty good at it! If there is a ghost in that dog house, I will find it, and get rid of it!"

Chapter 3
Something is Found

At a quarter till midnight, Jaba appeared at the fence, struggling again to pull himself under. He shook off the dirt collected from his crawl and drool flew in every direction. A tiny little giggle was heard from the dog house. Jaba slowly moved over to the door. He stuck his head inside to take a look. The big bulldog waited for his eyes to adjust to the thick darkness. Jaba didn't move a muscle. He smelled the musty dirt odor once again. The bulldog saw a little shadow move deep inside the dog house. He fumbled for his biggest and brightest flashlight, finally found it, and flashed it in the farthest corner. Standing in the light was a little grayish black furry animal with a long snout and sharp claws for hands. It had beady eyes almost completely covered with fur. The creature tried to

move away from the light, but the ghost hunter's big beam caught its every move.

"I gotcha," barked Jaba. "Don't think you can run away from me, you little ghost!"

The small dark figure cleared its throat and said, "Oh, did I scare you? I did not mean to scare you." And then laughed a tiny little laugh, "Te he he he."

The big dog bellowed. "Well, you didn't scare me, but you sure have my Spaniel friends worried. Are you the one responsible for all the noises coming out of this dog house?"

"Yes sir, I believe I am. Could you please turn off that light? I'm not used to seeing much of any kind of light."

"What are you doing in this dog house anyway?" Jaba demanded.

"Well, you see, I usually live under the ground, but I decided to live here for a change. It seemed like a great place. It's very dark and protects me from all the weather. The rustic style of it really suits me. I even brought in my own piles of dirt for burrowing. I really love what I've done with the place."

Jaba looked more carefully with the flashlight and noticed several mounds of dirt piled around inside the dog house.

"That's very interesting: a scavenger with a

sense of style. My name is Jaba the Mutt, but most folks just call me Jaba. What is your name?"

"Moe the Mole is my name, but you may call me Moe. I am very pleased to meet you, Mr. Jaba."

"So you're a mole?'

"Yes sir, please don't eat me."

"Oh, don't you worry Moe, I'm on a strict diet. I only eat my low-carb diet dog food. I'm trying to shed a few pounds."

Just then, Daisy, Joe, and Maggie came bolting through the doggie door of their owner's home. They heard the voices and wondered what was happening.

Chapter 4
The Ghost has a Story

"Have you found a ghost? Is our house haunted?" Maggie asked.

"Well, I think I found your ghost, and it's no ghost at all. Maggie, Joe, and Daisy, meet Moe." Jaba shined his big flashlight on Moe's tiny body as he stood in the doorway of their dog house. The Spaniels stared at the creature.

Moe crept out of the bright light and said, "Te he he he, I hope I didn't scare you too much."

Maggie barked, "You had us plenty scared, you little mouse."

"I beg your pardon madam, but I am no mouse. Moles are often confused for mice or rats, but actually, we are part of the burrowing mammal family."

"Well, we are the Spaniel family and we say,

GET OUT OF OUR DOG HOUSE!"

Moe quickly asked, "Maggie, are you not aware that dogs are also mammals? So, we could be related. Maybe we are distant cousins."

Maggie said, "Even if what you say is true, you didn't get permission before you inhabited our home."

"Oh, I'm so sorry, but your place is so nice, and as I was telling Mr. Jaba, it's rustic and dark and that's what I like."

Daisy asked, "How long have you been living in our home?"

"I have been here long enough to know quite a lot about you three dogs. I know Daisy likes to sneak off with everyone's bones and then she buries them right next to the loose board in your fence. She is so clever because the smell of the bones helps her to locate the special loose board that is your passageway to all of your adventures. I know Joe loves to chase squirrels around the yard and is the local paper delivery dog. He is getting really famous with his singing and song writing. Maggie loves to read and take long naps. She sometimes gets angry at her brother and sister dogs when they wake her. Big sister Maggie is always trying to keep her little siblings from getting into trouble. Why, just the other day, you warned Joe and Daisy to stay away from the skunk who was poking its nose under the fence."

Joe said, "Wow, you sure do know a lot about us! Your eyes are so tiny and covered with fur, how did you see all of this?"

"Excellent question, Joe. I have very little sight, but I can hear and smell very well and that is how I find out all of my information."

Daisy barked, "Well, that's all very interesting. But, you better watch what you say about me. I just might decide to eat you for a midnight snack!"

"I wouldn't do that if I were you."

"Why not?"

"Don't you know moles are likely to cause indigestion and gas? Instead, why don't you let me tell you a terribly interesting tale about your town?"

The Spaniel family looked at each other and agreed a story would be fun. Besides, they weren't getting any sleep with all the excitement going on in their backyard.

Chapter 5
A Spooky Tale

Moe sat down in one of his piles of dirt away from the flashlight. Just outside the dog house, Jaba, Joe, Daisy, and Maggie perked their ears and waited silently for the small mammal to begin. He introduced his tale with a short poem.

"A story I will tell you
about your little town.
What will the doggies do
when they hear what I have found?"

Then he began his spooky story about a place near their home.

"Years ago there was a very wealthy family who owned a large house on acres and acres of wooded, lush land. A most unusual stone fence surrounded their property. The rocks were uneven in size and had jagged edges that were mortared at different angles into the structure. It was a mosaic of odd shapes and dull, dead colors. The fence must have looked old even when it was first built."

Joe interrupted, and asked, "Does that house and the stone fence still exist?"

Moe scratched the dirt and dug out of his dirt pile. He crept closer to the dog house door saying, "The house was abandoned many years ago and parts of it are still standing, but most of it is gone. The fence, despite its old and odd appearance, is still there. Many believe the original owner and his wife are buried somewhere on the property. It is also rumored that strange things happen regularly out there."

"What kind of things?" Joe asked.

"Well, the remains of the house cast eerie shadows and some have sworn to have seen balls of light swoop and stop very briefly in the skeletal structure of the home. Also, in the woods, tiny blinking lights are seen piercing the darkness at certain times of the year. And then, there is the really scary part of the property!" Moe crawled a

little closer to the door.

Daisy barked, "Hey, let's go see it!"

Maggie said, "Be still now and listen to the story."

Then Moe said, "Actually, Daisy, that's not a bad idea. I think all of you can really experience the story better by following me."

Before Maggie could protest, Daisy followed Moe and led the dogs to the loose board in their fence. Daisy, Joe, and a reluctant Maggie climbed out. Jaba decided to try the loose board exit by squeezing through the opening. Moe dug a hole and tunneled.

The mole popped out of his tunnel on the other side of the fence and exclaimed,

"Follow me to the mystery
behind the jagged fence!
A house with lots of history
and none of it makes sense!"

Maggie stopped in her tracks and said, "I don't know about this. If we were frightened by a tiny mole, there is no telling how scared we'll be of what he is about to show us."

Jaba barked, "Now don't you worry, I'll protect you. I have my entire ghost hunting ensemble of equipment with me. We'll get to the bottom of this."

"Well, I suppose I should trust you with all of your experience."

"He looks trustworthy to me," said Joe.

Moe exclaimed, "Great! Let's go! You take the streets and I'll dig my way there."

Maggie said, "Jaba why don't you ride with me in our reliable red wagon. I can't walk very far and the wagon is a safe and fun way to go. This is how I go on all our adventures. Daisy and Joe will be happy to push and pull us. Won't you pups?"

Joe and Daisy looked at each other. They shook their heads while their ears dropped and their tails tucked. Maggie's siblings reluctantly said, "Okay." Then Daisy got behind the wagon to push and Joe went to the front to pull.

Joe said, "Come on Jaba, jump in. Let's get going."

Jaba slowly climbed in with his backpack of equipment and said, "Why thank you very much. Now I can save my energy for the investigation."

Off they went down their street to the mysterious property with the old stone fence. Joe puffed and grunted as he pulled and so did Daisy as she pushed the wagon. The extra weight of Jaba made the pups work very hard.

"How far is it?" Daisy asked while trying to catch her breath.

The mole popped his head out of the ground long enough to say, "Not too far, only about a mile."

Joe paused and panted saying, "Thank goodness. I'm already exhausted, but I can't wait to see this place. It sounds so spooky."

Chapter 6
The Whispering Fence

The Spaniels and Jaba followed Moe in the moonlight keeping their eyes fixed on his path. They could tell exactly where the underground mammal was by the long ruts and the occasional mounds of dirt he made along the way. The yards in the Spaniel family's neighborhood would never be the same after this midnight adventure. Finally, after much effort on Joe and Daisy's part, and many tunnels on Moe's part, they arrived at the stone fence.

The dogs crept along the fence while Moe surfaced. The old stone structure seemed to be whispering something to them. The dogs perked their ears and tried to listen. They thought they heard, "Stay away, stay away, stay away." The fence was repeating those words to them in a soft

voice with the tiniest little squeak. Everybody thought they heard it.

Maggie barked, "Let's get out of here, now!"

Jaba pulled out a special EVP (electronic voice phenomena) recorder. He told everyone, "My special equipment can magnify the faintest noises. Like the sounds that only a ghost can make and animals and people can barely hear, or can't hear at all." Then Jaba asked the fence, "Can you please speak to us again?" Everyone was completely still; there wasn't a sound anywhere. They waited and wondered. Finally, Jaba checked his tape and found nothing had been recorded. The bulldog said, "Well, maybe it was just the wind or something." He put his device away.

They continued along the stone fence toward the entrance. They heard the faint frightening words again, "Stay away, stay away, stay away."

Maggie started to shake all over. Moe listened very carefully. He announced to the dogs, "I think

I have solved the mystery of the whispering fence. You see, it is not whispering at all. I believe you have a wheel on your red wagon that needs some grease. Te he he he. If you noticed, whenever we stop the wagon, the whispering sound with the slight squeak stops, and whenever we move the wagon, it starts again. Te he he he."

Jaba thought about this for a second and then said, "Well, I do believe you're right. You are a clever little creature."

Moe said, "Okay my curious canine friends.

Just ahead you will see
the entrance to the property.
Far inside we must go
to the scariest place I know."

Chapter 7
Jaba is Frightened

Inside the fence, the dogs pushed through thick brush to find the old remains of the house. Finally, they saw the fragments of the fractured home. There, in the glow of the full moon, was an old fireplace and a foundation. A few walls were still standing and some pillars remained out front where a grand porch once stood. They saw a skeleton of what used to be a mansion on wooded, lush land. It was an eerie sight.

The animals stood very still to see if any balls of light would swoop and stop on the structure. They saw nothing. Then, they looked into the dark woods for the blinking lights. Jaba thought he saw a speck of light flash off to his left. He jerked his giant head in that direction, but the tiny light was gone. He stared into the dark woods and then it happened again, a flash of flickering light.

"Did you see that?" he asked.

The mole and the Spaniels were right next to him and they all whispered, "Yes."

Once more the light quickly appeared and then disappeared. Jaba crept into the forest and noticed even more tiny, blinking lights. He peered into the darkness and thought for a little while about what he was seeing. "Fireflies," he announced. "That flickering of lights is just a bunch of fireflies. Yep, that has to be it, the farther you go into the forest the more fireflies you see. Mystery solved!"

Then Jaba added, "As far as the balls of light swooping and stopping briefly on the remains of this house, well, I've been thinking about that too. Through the woods, right over there, I noticed this property is on a street corner. So, I think the balls of light are really just headlights shining over this structure as the cars turn the corner. I'm pretty certain that's what it is. My favorite thing to do with my ghost busting skills is to debunk these supposedly scary things."

Maggie said, "Oh, Jaba, you are so clever. Thank you for solving the mystery about this creepy place. Now let's go home."

Moe quickly stated, "Maybe it's true about the fireflies and the headlights, but one can never be one hundred percent sure. Te he he he." Then he added, "Maggie, remember we still haven't seen the scariest place of all."

"Yeah, let's go see it!" Joe and Daisy said.

The mole led them to a hole in the ground beside the foundation of the house that looked like an abandoned cellar. A beaten and battered old door stood open on a broken frame. The animals peered into an opening the size of a small doorway. In the moonlight they could barely see the dirt floor with the steep decline surrounded by old stone walls. The passageway appeared to lead to total darkness.

Moe warned, “I wouldn’t go down there if I were you. I have seen some strange things moving around in there. I believe there are ghosts and spooky things in that dark cavern.”

Then Maggie urged, “Well, nobody knows more about dark underground places better than a mole. I say we take his advice and skedaddle right now!”

But, before Maggie could leave, Jaba, Joe, and Daisy were all starting to go down into the cellar.

“Now there’s no need for all three of us to go,” said Jaba. “I’m the ghost expert here, let me go first.”

Jaba moved slowly into the dark dungeon with his ghost detecting equipment. The air was extremely fragrant with an even thicker, dirtier smell than the Spaniel family’s dog house. Jaba had strange feelings about his surroundings. He thought he heard something scratching and thumping. He stopped to listen and the sounds stopped.

Was his mind playing tricks on him? He couldn't be sure. Jaba felt his way along and did not turn on his flashlight. The ghost hunter was trying to sneak up on whatever was down there, and he knew the light would scare it away. The bulldog had investigated many places, but this one was making his skin crawl and his fur stand up. He felt something brush up against his face. Jaba let out a quick snort and stood very still. He sniffed the air and nudged his nose just a little bit forward and felt something crawl onto it. Looking cross-eyed into the darkness, he finally saw a spider. The big dog realized he had run into a spider's web. Jaba shook the creepy crawly creature off of his nose.

The bulldog carefully crept farther into the dark cavern. It was the blackest place he had ever been. He could see nothing but felt something surround him. Jaba finally turned on his smallest flashlight. The ghost hunter saw a very scary sight that made him gasp and jump.

He made the quickest turn a bulldog has ever made and ran out of the opening of the cellar.

Maggie, Joe, Daisy, and Moe watched as Jaba gathered himself to explain.

He finally caught his breath and blurted, "There are fresh graves down there...a whole bunch of them. There is just one mound after another."

"I told you it was scary!" exclaimed Moe.

All the dogs ran back to their wagon at the stone fence. Moe dug his way out and joined them. They all rushed back to the Spaniel family's backyard. They had seen and heard enough! Once they arrived at the Spaniel's home, they just sat and tried to catch their breath.

"I'm exhausted," announced Maggie. "I'm going to bed. If you want to, Moe, you may sleep in our dog house. I'm too afraid to sleep outside." She went through the doggie door, but Joe and Daisy did not follow her.

Joe said, "I sure do wish we could figure out

why those graves are down there and who they belong to. Maybe we should call the Texas Rangers to come and help us."

Then Daisy said, "Well, I'm certainly not going to let what Jaba found down in the cellar keep me from going back. I love a good mystery and I bet we can solve this one!"

"In all my paranormal moments I have never been so perplexed or frightened, but I will gather my courage and go back there tomorrow, if you guys will go with me," announced Jaba.

A tiny little "Te he he he," came out of Moe's mouth. Then he said:

"Tomorrow we will see
how brave you dogs will be.
Now we go to bed
with images we dread."

Chapter 8
The Fear Spreads

The next morning, Maggie read the Greyhound Gazette as she does every morning. She found some very interesting news stories.

Just beside the article about how to get rid of gophers and moles in your yard and garden, was a series of reports about the odd happenings in several of the town's most important buildings. The news was interesting, mysterious, and scary.

Apparently, there had been weird things happening all over town. For example, at the hospital, the plumbing stopped working and banging noises had been heard in their basement. At the courthouse, trials had been halted because of the odd scratching sounds and the vibrations people felt under their feet.

Even the newspaper office had experienced thumping and digging noises. Each of these locations reported hearing faint laughter accompanying the other sounds.

Rumors were flying and tongues were wagging. The town was convinced there was something going on underneath it, and many believed their little town was haunted. The Sheriff and police were responding as quickly as possible to all of the calls from the citizens. They even thought about calling the Texas Rangers. Maggie showed the articles to Joe and Daisy. Then she called Jaba to report the news.

Meanwhile, Moe was burrowed in a big pile of dirt in their dog house and was sleeping a very peaceful sleep.

Joe ran over to the dog house door and barked, "Hey, get up in there, we have important news!"

The mole dug his way out, briefly stuck his head up, and said, "I'll see you in a minute after I

have my morning grub."

Once everyone had been informed of the stories circulating throughout their community, Maggie announced, "Something has got to be done about what Jaba found in the cellar!" Everyone eagerly agreed with her. They knew they had to go back out there and try to solve this mystery. They made a plan to meet at half-past eleven that night to go to the scary property.

Chapter 9
Mystery Solved

Everyone made it safely to the opening of the cellar. At first, nobody wanted to go inside. They just stood there waiting for someone to be brave. Finally, Daisy decided things were going way too slowly. The little black dog darted down the dark passageway. Jaba and Joe quickly followed. Maggie carefully crept into the cellar.

Jaba barked, "Hey, Daisy, wait for us. I have all the equipment we need."

Daisy was already deep in the dungeon and saw something scurry across the dirt floor. She froze in her tracks, and then, her curiosity made her snoop some more. Daisy barked back to her followers, "I found something! Hurry up with that flashlight! I think I spotted a ghost down here!"

Then Joe ran right into Daisy. They both

jumped, half scared to death, and began barking and howling. Jaba joined in the noise making and Maggie chimed in as well. Moe was still waiting at the cellar entrance. None of them could hear him, but he was laughing his silly little, "Te he he he."

Once the barking and howling ceased, Jaba caught up to Daisy and Joe and shined his big flashlight. All around them were piles of dirt with gopher heads popping out of each one. The gophers and dogs stared at each other in the bright flashlight.

Jaba exclaimed, "I'll be doggoned!" There's no graveyard down here! It's just a bunch of gopher mounds!"

Joe and Daisy began chasing the furry little "grave diggers", but they were too quick. They ran down their holes well out of the Spaniel's reach. The gophers continued their tunneling under the town.

At the top of the cellar, Moe could be heard laughing, "Te he he he," the loudest they had ever heard him.

The dogs came out of the dungeon with their tails tucked. They were so embarrassed at how they had been tricked by the mischievous mole. Moe couldn't stop laughing at how he had fooled his new friends. Finally, he stopped and said, "I was just playing a prank on you pups."

Maggie scolded Moe saying, "You really had us frightened with all your stories about this place. You ought to be ashamed of yourself!"

"Yes, I know. I was planning to tell you the truth but you believed everything I told you and it was so funny. Te he he he." Then Moe looked at each dog with his most sincere expression saying, "Please forgive me. I really am sorry."

The dogs began to laugh at how they had been fooled and they all forgave the little mole.

Then Moe cleared his throat and said to anybody who was listening that night:

"Don't believe everything you read or hear.
There could be an explanation for what you fear.
Stories and rumors can get out of hand.
Search for the truth and there you will stand."

Joe and Moe's Mystery Solved Song

To be sung to the tune of
"The Itsy Bitsy Spider"

Verse 1

Our dog house may be haunted,
we can't explain the sounds.
Jaba solved the mystery.
He found the little mounds.
Out popped a mole
from his tiny little hole
to tell our family
there's another mystery.

Say this... The mole told us

Verse 2

A creepy scary story
about your little town.
Many would be frightened
to hear what I have found.
You must follow me
to the old property.
Behind the jagged fence,
there's another mystery.

Verse 3

Could we believe our ears?
We had to go and see.
There was no time to waste.
Moe led us without haste.
We bravely faced our fears
in the deep dark tunnel place
where the Spaniel Family
solved the mystery.

Glossary

Basement: The floor in a building next to or below the principal floor.

Bellowed: To make a loud sound or roar.

Burrowed: To make a hole in the ground for shelter and habitation.

Cavern: An underground chamber, a cave.

Chimed: To make a sound in harmony or agreement.

Creature: A living created being that is either animal or human.

Debunk: To expose, remove, and disprove false or unproven claims.

Dungeon: An underground dark prison or vault.

Ensemble: All of the parts needed to make something complete.

Feverishly: Excitedly and with speed.

Fractured: Broken

Fragments: A small detached portion from the whole.

Grub: The thick wormlike larva of certain beetles and other insects. *Slang* for food.

Inhabited: To live in and occupy as a place of residence.

Mammal: A warm blooded animal, such as a human being, dog or whale, the female of which produces milk to feed her babies.

Massive: Large, weighty, and broad in scope.

Mischievous: Causing trouble or annoyance to others.

Mortared: Secured in place with a building material made from mixing cement with sand and water, and sometimes other materials.

Mosaic: A surface decoration made by securing small pieces of colored glass, stone, or other material in regular or random patterns.

Paranormal: An experience that does not have an obvious or scientific explanation and is considered beyond the range of normal experiences.

Perplexed: Filled with uncertainty; puzzled.

Phenomena: An extraordinary event known through the senses rather than by thought.

Reluctant: Unwilling or resisting.

Rustic: Refering to something that is plain, simple, and not polished. A rustic structure is usually made of rough irregular wood.

Scavenger: A person or animal who gathers things discarded or left by others.

Siblings: Individuals having one or both parents in common; a brother or sister.

Sincere: To be truthful, pure, and genuine.

Skedaddle: To leave quickly.

The Texas Rangers: Officers of the law who protect our great state of Texas and all of us. They still wear boots, white hats, and pistol belts.

Trickling: A slow, small, irregular flow.

Works Cited

Holroyd, Jill, and Miles S. Holroyd. "Moles and Molecatchers." The Dumvilles of Hunton. 11 Nov. 2007. 31 July 2008 <http://www.dumville.org/moles.html>.

"How to Kill Moles & Gophers." EPest Supply. 1997. 24 Nov. 2008 < http://www.epestsupply.com/moles.htm>.

"Mole." Wikipedia, The Free Encyclopedia. 27 Apr. 2002. 31 July 2008 <http://en.wikipedia.org/wiki/Mole>.

Pierce, Robert A. "G 9940 Controlling Nuisance Moles MU Extension." University of Missouri Extension.1993. 30 July 2008 <http://extension.missouri.edu/xplor/agguides/wildlife/g09440.htm>.

Schmieg, Sebastian. "Itsy Bisty Spider." Kid Songs. 26 July 2006. 26 Oct. 2008 <http://kidsongs.wordpress.com/2006/08/15/itsy-bitsy-spider/>.

Dogs make great pets.

The Spaniel Family highly recommends visiting your local animal shelter, humane society, or rescue group to adopt a wonderful dog.

Here are a few websites:

SPCA of Texas
www.spca.org

Humane Society of North Texas
www.hsnt.org

Humane Society of Southeast Texas
www.petsforpeople.org

American Kennel Club Springer Spaniel National Website
http://www.akc.org/breeds/english_springer_spaniel/index.cfm

English Springer Rescue America
www.springerrescue.org

American Spaniel Club National Website
www.asc-cockerspaniel.org

Cocker Spaniel Rescue of East Texas-Houston
www.cockerkids.org

Cocker Spaniel Rescue of Dallas and Ft. Worth
www.dfwcockerrescue.org

Cocker Spaniel Rescue of Austin & San Antonio
www.austincockerrescue.org

At the age of four, Sharon Ellsberry was the youngest child in her neighborhood. When all of her playmates went off to school, Sharon had to use her imagination to find things to do. She really wanted to go to school, so she decided to hold "dog school" in the basement of her childhood home. With a box of treats she rounded up neighborhood dogs, then sneaked the dogs into the basement and played "dog school." From that early time, Sharon developed a love for animals and using her imagination.

After earning a Bachelor of Arts from the University of Houston, Sharon had a successful career in marketing for over twenty years. Then she began to yearn to do something with the stories she had been writing. In 2003, she started the journey to take her Spaniel Family stories into publication. To date, Sharon has authored three children's books: *The Mystery of the Spaniel Family's Dog House*, *The Spaniel Family's Pen Pal Adventure* and *The Spaniel Family Goes to the State Fair*. She is working on two more books about the Spaniel Family that will be in publication in the coming years. In all of her stories she weaves the threads of childhood fantasies and the joy of being with animals.

Sharon is a member of the Society of Children's Book Writers and Illustrators, and participates in several writers critique groups. She enjoys presenting her books with her creative storytelling and skits. Sharon has done numerous programs for schools, libraries, bookstores, and organizations. To learn more about her programs and the Spaniel Family visit www.gospaniels.com.

Growing up in an artistic family, Amy Fox has always been interested in all things creative. She ran her first business in fourth grade creating and selling small furry animals with the help of her best friend and her mom. In high school she began making jewelry, which led to her degree in Jewelry Design from the University of North Texas.

When Amy met Judy Bell, the owner of a teacher's supply store, she was told that a local author was looking for an illustrator and was asked if she would be interested. Amy was very interested and looked forward to the chance to illustrate a book, something she had always wanted to do.

Amy worked closely with Sharon over several months to complete the illustrations for *The Spaniel Family's Pen Pal Adventure.* She worked with Sharon again on her latest book *The Mystery of the Spaniel Family's Dog House.* Amy has also completed illustrations for two other books by another North Texas author.